THE DONKEY IN THE LIVING ROOM

A tradition that celebrates
the true meaning of Christmas

Sarah Raymond Cunningham

with illustrations by Michael Foster

KIDS

Nashville, Tennessee

Dewey Decimal Classification: J232.92

Subject Heading: CHRISTMAS \ JESUS CHRIST–NATIVITY \ CHRISTMAS STORIES

ISBN: 978-1-4336-8317-6

Printed in China

1 2 3 4 5 6 7 8 • 18 17 16 15 14

To Justus, Malachi, Grace,
Abby, Baby Kovacs-Raymond,
and Baby Bailey-Raymond

The people who live in darkness have seen a great light,
and for those living in the shadowland of death,
light has dawned. —MATTHEW 4:16

An Invitation:

When I was a little girl, a donkey arrived in the living room exactly nine days before Christmas. *But it wasn't just any donkey.*

Every morning after my brothers and I rolled out of bed, we would scramble to the living room where a tiny package wrapped in Christmas paper would be waiting on our mantel. When our little fingers ripped through the wrapping, we'd uncover a figurine from the family nativity scene: a donkey or Mary or perhaps, as we neared Christmas Day, an angel. After we uncovered the figurine, we would race to our dad, crawl up on his lap, and he would tell us an enchanted holiday story from long, long ago. *And he would tell it from the point of view of the figurine we placed in his hands.* As the days passed, we gradually collected the pieces of Christ's birthday story.

When we got old enough, Dad began to let us tell the parts of the stories we knew. Looking back now, I realize that the real gift was never the figurines we unwrapped. *The gift was the story.* And now that my brothers and I have children of our own, we too give the gift of story to our own children as we gather around the nativity each Christmas.

I want to invite you and your family into this tradition, to have your children unwrap the nativity figurines along with us each day leading up to Christmas. It is my hope that your children and grandchildren will pass down this tradition, as my family has, and that families across the world will continue to gather around the gift of story at Christmas.

How To:

1. A couple of weeks before Christmas, wrap each figurine of your nativity scene. If there is a group of figurines, such as shepherds or kings, wrap all of them together in one package. Label them so you know what each package holds.

2. Place the figurine scheduled to be unwrapped in the same place every day, so the kids will know where to rush to find them each morning. A mantel, coffee table, or favorite chair will work great! If you miss a day or start late, you can always do more than one reading each day. Even if you receive this book as a gift on Christmas Day, you could wrap all the figurines and place them, in order, in various rooms of your house to be found and read all on the same day!

   9 Days Before Christmas – Mary, Mother of Jesus

   8 Days Before Christmas – The Donkey

   7 Days Before Christmas – The Cow

   6 Days Before Christmas – The Sheep

   5 Days Before Christmas – The Shepherd

   4 Days Before Christmas – The Angel

   3 Days Before Christmas – The Camel

   2 Days Before Christmas – The Wise Men

   1 Day Before Christmas – Joseph, Father of Jesus

   Christmas Day – Baby Jesus

3. Let the kids find and unwrap the figurine assigned to the day. Then allow them to hold it while you read the corresponding story on the pages that follow.

Most of all, take your time, welcome questions, and enjoy creating this eternally important Christmas tradition with your family.

MARY, MOTHER OF JESUS

Have you heard about little miss Mary?
Not the one with the lamb or the one contrary,
But the one who lived a long time before.
To begin this great story, she will tell you more.

In the days just before taxes were due,
A visitor came to me, right out of the blue.
An angel appeared, and there, standing tall,
Gabriel gave me the news that started it all.

"You're going to have a baby!" he cried.
I worried and I trembled; I shook and I sighed.
"But don't be afraid," he told me just then,
"God favors you, Mary, among women and men."

"How can this be?" I asked the winged being.
I couldn't believe what I was hearing and seeing!
"God's Spirit will help you; you will give birth,
And the boy who is born, He will save the whole earth."

Even though part of me wanted to run,
I said, "I am God's servant, so let this be done."

THE **DONKEY**

Have you heard of the famed donkey of old?
The load that he carried was worth way more than gold.
Other donkeys knew he wasn't the same;
He will tell us now how he earned his donkey fame.

When I was young, Augustus was Caesar.
Believe me, his census was not a crowd pleaser.
We had to hightail it to our hometowns,
So the rulers could count us and write our names down.

To make their trips a bit quicker, of course,
People saddled a donkey or camel or horse.
Out of all the people, Mary's husband-to-be
Waltzed into the stable and picked little old me.

We loaded up and left Galilee fast;
Joseph was related to a king from the past.
King David had been from a far-off land,
So we all had to hoof it through grass, rock, and sand.

It wasn't easy, tracking through the dust,
But my mind was made up: to Bethlehem or bust!

8 DAYS until Christmas

THE COW

Have you ever heard where the donkey stopped,
As Mary's belly was getting ready to pop?
To fill you in, we'll now cut to the cow;
She's the best one to tell you the who, what, and how.

One dark night, I heard the clickity-clack
Of a donkey arriving and loosening his pack.
A bearded man sauntered up to the inn
And announced that he'd come to the land of his kin.

"We've got no room here," the innkeeper said,
"You can sleep in the stable; we don't have a bed."
Mary came in and sat by the manger,
And then after that, the night got even stranger.

Joseph was pacing, his face in a frown,
And Mary was hurting, so she had to lie down.
We all stayed quiet, not even mooing,
As everyone sensed something big was now brewing.

And sure enough, when we woke the next morn,
We could see, plain as day, a baby had been born.

THE **SHEEP**

Have you heard about the dazed hillside flock,
Who were greeted one night with the shock of all shocks?
Here to tell it is a sheep from that field.
Listen closely now—he's got a story to wield.

Back then, whenever it grew dark at night,
The shepherds made sure to keep all us sheep in sight.
They paced around to prevent any scares
From lions or wolves or even big, hairy bears.

There I was standing in the dark, pitch black,
When a ripple of *baa*-ing broke out in the pack.
Each sheep was staring straight up to the sky,
As a bright light and loud noise erupted on high.

The shepherds were afraid—it was easy to hear—
But the words that were said from the sky calmed their fears.
Instead of letting us sleep for a bit,
They packed up our stuff and led us off on a trip.

Soon, we all joined an odd celebration
For one little baby who brought us salvation.

6 DAYS until Christmas

THE **SHEPHERD**

Have you heard that the men watching their sheep
Saw a light in the sky while the world was asleep?
This guy tells you what the light was about
And why they decided to pack up and head out.

We were carefully keeping watch by night,
When the sheep began *baa*-ing and bleating in fright!
It was the strangest thing we'd seen, by far,
Every one of our sheep looking up at the stars.

I saw one herder turn white as the snow;
I thought, sure enough, I'd be the next one to go.
I was pale as wool; my knees were shaking
At the humming and drumming the sky was making.

Then a voice cried out, "Do not be afraid!"
And before I could faint, an announcement was made.
Something big was happening right down the road.
To investigate more, we all packed up our loads.

We rounded the herd, took off straightaway,
And flocked to the stable where the lone baby lay.

THE ANGEL

Have you heard how angels lit up the sky
And delivered a message from our God on high?
I could tell you about a night so good,
But if anyone should tell you, an angel should.

It was dark and black all over the place—
Why, you couldn't see your wing in front of your face!
Then I appeared, in God's glorious light,
And those frightened shepherds almost died at the sight.

"Good news!" I said. "The Messiah is here!"
(That's when every last angel came out and appeared.)
We sang and praised God again and again,
Saying, "Glory to God! Peace and goodwill to men!"

The shepherds didn't know *what* had just hit,
But you should have seen how fast they got up and split!
As soon as I'd said the last of the news,
They were herding their sheep, grabbing staffs, coats,
    and shoes!

After that night, it was just as you'd bet:
They told the story to every person they met.

THE CAMEL

Have you heard of the camel from afar,
Trudging along to follow a big, sparkly star?
I could tell you and go out on a limb,
But I think we ought to leave the story to him.

My master came in, back home in the East.
He said, "Let us get going, my trustworthy beast.
The words of the ancients are coming true,
And I'd like to be there to see it, wouldn't you?"

To honor a king, the grandest of grand,
He packed only the finest of things from our land.
He piled up the gold, shiny and yellow,
And the best myrrh that you could find for a fellow.

There was frankincense, too, with its rich scent,
But I had no idea what all these gifts meant.
I knew this king must be worth the trouble,
'Cause my master and friends left town on the double.

I knew something huge would happen that day;
It was the only time that a star lit our way!

THE WISE MEN

Have you heard of the group of men so wise,
They traveled to Jerusalem as the crow flies?
I could take their story down from the shelf—
Better yet, I'll let a wise man tell you himself.

We'd been studying the sky late one night,
When one star became crazy, amazingly bright.
It was a sign! A king was on His way!
So we made plans to leave on that very same day.

We rode to Jerusalem, miles and miles,
To ask King Herod about the coming Christ child.
The king called his priests and teachers of law,
And he wasn't happy with what he heard and saw.

From Bethlehem town this ruler would rise.
"Go," Herod told us, "find the baby where He lies."
We tracked the star to right over the boy,
And the hearts of we wise men were filled with pure joy.

God told us in dreams not to trust Herod;
We never went back to the palace to share it.

2 DAYS until Christmas

JOSEPH, FATHER OF JESUS

Have you heard of Jesus' earthly dad?
Joseph can tell you of the adventures he had.
If you've been wondering when he'd take the scene,
We won't delay! We'll let him now spill what he's seen!

When Mary's tummy first started to grow,
There is one thing that happened, you really should know.
An angel told me, "Stay with sweet Mary;
She's been given a gift from God she must carry."

In Bethlehem, just as the others said,
Our baby was born with a manger for His bed.
Shepherds did visit, and wise men to boot,
And angels whose voices were as smooth as a flute.

Yes, Herod wanted to hurt our new son,
So we fled to Egypt, taking Him on the run.
God warned us to go, again through a dream.
He was always there watching over us, it seemed.

Our son grew up to die and rise again,
To complete God's great gift of goodwill for all men.

BABY JESUS

Now we have come to the baby so small,
The one with the most important story of all.
If there's just one that you make time to hear,
Let it be Jesus' story, this Christmas, my dear.

The stories are true, what everyone saw;
I was born in a stable, surrounded by straw,
Wrapped in swaddling clothes, laid in a manger,
Among my family and an odd group of strangers.

But more importantly, the rest is true:
That I came out of God's love for each one of you.
I am Immanuel, God with you from birth,
The awaited Messiah who shepherds the earth.

John 10 says I came so you'd have full life;
In John 16, I promised I'd overcome strife.
I stood against wrong and set people free,
Preached good for the poor and helped blind people
     to see.

One thing to take from this story above
Is that Mine is a story of absolute love,
Of hope and of truth, of life and of light.
It's a story for all year—not just Christmas night.

In all the hoopla, buying, and selling,
Remember that *this* is the story worth telling.

Remember:

"I proclaim to you good news of great joy that will be for all the people." –*Luke 2:10*

Read:

In Luke 2:25–35, you'll meet a man named Simeon. After Jesus was born, His parents took Him to the temple to be dedicated, and Simeon was there. He took Jesus into his arms and told Mary and Joseph that he had been waiting to meet their newborn baby, the Savior of the world. Mary and Joseph were amazed by what he said. How many people do you know who are just waiting to meet Jesus? Christmas—when we celebrate Jesus' entry into this world—is the perfect time to introduce others to Him!

Think:

1. Which character in Jesus' story is your favorite? Why?
2. Why do you think God chose a stable as Jesus' birth place?
3. Why is it important that we share Jesus' story?
4. How has His story changed your life?
5. Who do you know that needs to hear His story?

Do:

Give the gift of God's story.

1. Tear around the edges of a sheet of white paper to make it look distressed.
2. Using a paint brush and cooled coffee, "paint" the paper and allow it to dry. (This will give the paper an old, yellowed look.)
3. On the paper, draw or write (or both!) the story of Christmas in your own words, in your own way.
4. Roll up the paper like a scroll, and tie it with a ribbon.
5. Give the story of Jesus to someone for Christmas.

Share the story of Jesus—at Christmas and all year long!